Leanne Shapton

Toys Talking

Enfant

drawnandquarterly.com

First edition: October 2017
Printed in China
10 9 8 7 6 5 4 3 2 1

Library and Archives Canada Cataloguing in Publication. Shapton, Leanne, author, illustrator. *Toys Talking* / Leanne Shapton. ISBN 978-1-77046-298-4 (hardcover) I. Title. PS8637.H369T69 2017 jC813'.6 C2017-901678-4. Published in the USA by Drawn & Quarterly, a client publisher of Farrar, Straus and Giroux. Orders: 888.330.8477. Published in Canada by Drawn & Quarterly, a client publisher of Raincoast Books. Orders: 800.663.5714.

 Drawn & Quarterly acknowledges the support of the Government of Canada and the Canada Council for the Arts for our publishing program.

for Tomasina

Never mind that,
come as you are.

It is not pleasant to travel in such weather.

He is very touchy.

I have often had sleepless nights.

I shall think it over.

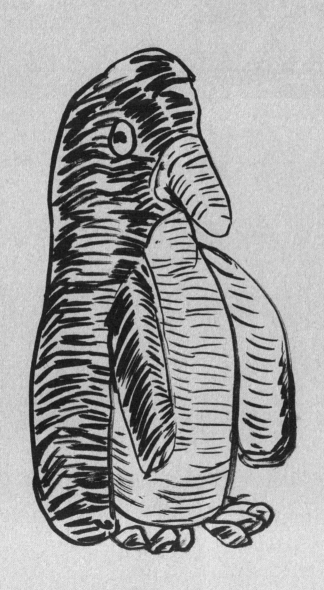

She has no manners.

I long for tomorrow
to come.

You are rather
too particular.

All my evenings
are engaged.

He dines out
nearly every day.

That is no concern
of ours.

You are wrong to be angry with me.

Tell me your troubles.

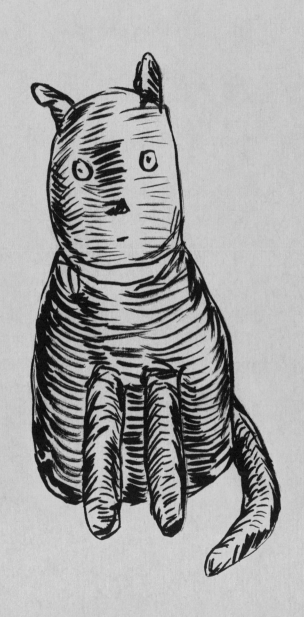

You must hear
both sides.

You are joking.

We can not afford it.

She is very clever.

He does his best.

She has a large
appetite.

We are among friends.